FROM ERIK'S DIARY
(LORELAI AND I)

EPISODE 3

SEARCHING HERE
SEARCHING THERE

I0533268

Massimo Indrio

© Massimo Indrio
www.massimoindrio.com
first edition: november 2014
ISBN: 978-88-940304-2-6
Translation by Brett Auerbach-Lynn

CHAPTER 1

Someone - I can't remember whom at the moment - had advised me not to invest in Pickled Vegetables and Associates, Inc. but as usual, I didn't listen. So when the renowned chef Gaston Tourtel, recognized - wrongly in my eyes - as the universal arbiter of culinary good taste, suggested pickled vegetables be avoided like the plague, the value of my stocks plummeted to the point that I was barely able to exchange them for a coffee machine at the flea market.

Now I'm not saying I didn't need a new coffee machine, quite the contrary. But for what it had cost me, it should at the very least have been made of solid gold.

Despite this blow I didn't lose my cool, for I had long since learned not to get too upset when things didn't go my way.

Lorelai, on the other hand, hadn't taken it quite so well. But this was also because at first she hadn't understood exactly what had happened. I'm not sure how, but she somehow understood that I'd lost the photos from our last vacation on the Walrus Coast of Greenland, the memories of which were especially dear to her. I knew how she felt and I too would've been sorry to have lost them, particularly that photo she'd taken of me astride an elephant seal as I chased after a group of polar bears. It must be said – there've been times when I've acted like an absolute fool just so to impress that enchanting blond.

This little mix-up had made Lorelai a little upset. It was immediately evident because whenever she got upset, she always started softly singing a strange, calming lullaby of Bulgarian origin her grandmother had taught her.

Once we'd cleared up the misunderstanding, however, she began to laugh, embraced me, and promised I'd always be her adorable little sweetie pie, even if we ended up having to live under a bridge. Truthfully she didn't need to say it - I knew I could count on her. She certainly wasn't like the wife of my great-grandfather Amos, who'd left her husband merely because he'd lost the family castle in a passionate game of darts. Unlike Lorelai my great-grandmother was a woman who gave great importance to money, though at the time she'd declared that the cause of separation was my great-grandfather's habit of eating bread, onions, and garlic just before coming to bed. Truth be told, good old Amos wasn't the least bit displeased to be left alone, for he dreamed of thus regaining his long-lost freedom. But as soon as his wife got wind of this, she returned even quicker than she'd left, bringing along her elderly mother Genoveffa, a.k.a. the Harpy of Montecupo.

But that's neither here nor there. A sizeable portion of my wealth had thus, as they say, gone up in smoke, but as I mentioned I wasn't being overly dramatic. I could still count on various sources of income, not the least of which were the rights deriving from my famous treatise on the inutility of logical thought, an international bestseller that had been translated into every world language apart from English, Spanish, French and German.

Nevertheless I began to consider the possibility of setting off on a new, stimulating and profitable enterprise. I shared my thoughts with Lorelai but quickly regretted having done so because, in her candid naivety, she immediately started offering me the most bizarre advice. First, she suggested I go down to the hospital and offer my services as head neurosurgeon. Then - confessing that this was her favorite idea - she advised me to make a big-budget science-fiction film. As a last option, she proposed I run in the upcoming presidential election. I knew perfectly well that these off-the-wall ideas whirring around in her head were dictated by the great esteem she had for me, and though it was all very flattering, it was also quite unrealistic. I was used to keeping my feet firmly on the ground. What Lorelai didn't understand was that I wasn't looking for an actual job. The enterprise I had in mind was more along the lines of those of the Count of Monte Cristo, Aladdin, and Sinbad the sailor, men capable of filling their pockets from one day to the next by finding treasures, magic lamps and the like. While I knew these were only fictitious characters, my personality brought me in an altogether natural and spontaneous way to choose them as my role models.

As soon as I talked to her about it, Lorelai agreed that this was the right way to go. Seeing as we were now on the same wavelength, I thought the moment had come to celebrate. I put on some festive music, we opened two bottles of Arjavalos juice, and danced for a good half-hour (I only danced for about five minutes myself because, apart from certain ritual and hypnotic dances, I'm actually not a big fan of dancing, in and of itself).

CHAPTER 2

If my idea was to find a treasure, then there was only one obstacle left to overcome - where to find it? I needed to think it over for a while in peace and quiet, so I went into the purple study and sunk into the harlequin-patterned couch. As I gazed at the oil painting that depicted with great verisimilitude the wreck of the three-master *Old Valkyrie* against the legendary Lighthouse of Alexandria, I set myself to thinking about my next moves. I quickly came to the conclusion that I had to find myself a map or something similar and that the best place to look for one was in the library up in the tower, where for generations members of my family had accumulated volumes, manuscripts, letters, documents - and probably treasure maps as well. I nurtured especially high hopes for the diary of One-Eyed Buck, an ancestor of mine on the side of Grandma Fiammetta who had enjoyed some degree of success in the pirating profession during the 17th century. Famous for having invented the corkscrew grappling-iron and the retractable, squir-

ting saber, in his day One-Eyed Buck had ma-
rauded his way around the various seas and
oceans of the world, and it was not unlikely
that he'd hidden a few chests full of gold dou-
bloons under a couple of meters of sand so-
mewhere. My grandfather Gunnar, a reindeer
farmer in Scandinavia, had often told me about
him when I went to stay with him during
school vacations, and we spent long evenings
in front of the fireplace as the ferocious bliz-
zards outside prevented us from going out to
admire the *aurora borealis* or picnic on a block
of ice.

Satisfied with my conclusions, I left the study anxious to share them with Lorelai. But I
found a note in the entranceway, hanging from
the nose of a great wooden idol I'd brought
back from a recent trip to Oceania, that infor-
med me that she'd gone with her friend Domi-
tilla to see an exhibit of Neo-Parallelist, Post-
Cubist painters. Apart from my disappointment
in not finding her, attaching this note to the
nose of Rha-Ku-Tà (this being the name of the
idol) seemed a most disrespectful gesture towards the deity, despite our lack of familiarity
with him.

So I went back up to the library, winding my
way up the narrow steps that led to the top of
the tower, and began to dig in search of One-
Eyed Buck's diary.

Just how long *had* my ancestors been piling
up books and documents on those dusty shel-

ves? I came across medieval codices, scrolls scribbled in Latin, papyri full of hieroglyphics, and even stone blocks with cuneiform characters carved into them. After a good hour of searching, I finally found the long-awaited diary, its leather cover darkened by the passage of time and its pages yellowed, half-hidden behind a rare edition of an Assyro-Babylonian cookbook. As I read it I was immediately immersed in centuries past, a different world and a different time - an epoch in which human life frankly wasn't worth squat. The diary spoke in fact of assaults, battles, shipwrecks, plots, mutinies, executions, imprisonments, and great escapes. At times it even spoke of great passion and romance, but of treasure not a word. It was obvious that in his diary old Buck had prudently avoided any mention of his 'gains,' their value, and the location where he'd hidden them. Just the same, I continued reading because I found the diary extremely interesting. I want to refer just a couple of stories that seem particularly worth telling. The first is the account of how Buck lost his eye. During the boarding of another ship, a speck of dust had made its way into his eye and in order to get it out, he'd had the regrettable idea of asking the help of his boatswain Willy, a.k.a. the Hook. The second episode, rather, recounts the kidnapping of the Duchess of Culotte, a pestiferous French noblewoman who just wouldn't shut up. Buck and his crew kidnapped her one night in Maracaibo. But when they went to her husband to collect the ransom money, he offered them a cash reward if they would only take her with them.

Toward the end of the dairy, the old scallywag finally decided to talk about some chests full of gold and jewels he'd hidden in a cave on the Isle of Goats. My attention suddenly tripled. But soon after my hopes were dashed on the rocks when I read that Buck, now old and decrepit, sensing that death was upon him and wanting to save his soul, had had the brilliant idea of donating everything to a certain Countess Elena Freghieri of Arraffarraffa, who in return had promised to build a hospice for old, needy pirates.

What an inglorious end! Not his, mine.

In any case, as usual I didn't get too upset and went out to take a walk in the park before it got dark.

CHAPTER 3

It was a magnificent evening. The rays of light filtered through the leaves in the trees and bathed them in warm, golden light. I sat down on a bench and distractedly began to observe the few people who like me had decided to spend that last half-hour of light in the open air. Almost all of them were neighbors of ours. Among them I recognized the soprano Beatrice Ugolini, who so often delighted us with her interminable warbling; my painter-friend Robert, who on nights of a full moon turned into a werewolf; the homeless man, Henry, who slept in the middle of the park under the monument to Baron Munchausen; and Professor Giraldo, one of the first physicists to calculate how many drops it took to fill up a half-liter bottle.

I was thinking about practically nothing when I saw approaching, dressed as always in black, the lanky form of Miss Morty - profession psychic. I've never had any difficulty believing in the possibility of communication between this world and other dimensions. But I no longer had much respect for Miss Morty, ever since that time she'd confided to me that the ghost of Einstein had revealed to her during a séance that his famous $E=mc^2$ formula had been misunderstood. According to her, it really meant that an earache (E) is proportional (m) to the square of the number of crab cakes (c^2) consumed. Sincerely I found this a little difficult to swallow.

With all the free benches in the park, Miss Morty just had to sit down on the one next to mine. She politely said hello and told me, "You know Einstein got back in touch with me?"

"In touch?" I asked amazed.

"It's just a figure of speech. He confessed that the story about the earache and the crab cakes was just a gag. You know, he was famous for being quite the joker."

This statement restored my faith in Miss Morty. Now I could believe once more.

"I have a message for you," she continued.

"For me? From whom?"

"An ancestor of yours who says his name is One-Eyed Buck - a pirate, or so it would seem."

My interest was suddenly peaked, and with ears wide open I asked her to continue.

"Oh, there's not much to say. He just wanted me to tell you this: 'Break open the cover!'"

For a moment I didn't know what to say. Then I asked her: "Which cover? I have a lot of them at home."

"I wouldn't know. He didn't specify."

"Didn't he say anything else to you?"

"Well yes, in truth he said several other things, but they're my business and it would be completely inappropriate to repeat them," said Miss Morty, visibly blushing. "You know that ancestor of yours is quite the scoundrel? I do like him though. I certainly do like him!"

Having said this she got up, said goodbye, and walked away with that typically sinuous walk of hers that reminded you of a snake standing erect on his hind legs, if Mother Nature had ever produced such a thing.

I sat there for a few minutes thinking about all the different covers we had in the house. I thought about what Lorelai would've said. She'd surely think I'd gone crazy. And indeed, it had to be asked - what could possibly be the point of such an operation?

Just as I was immersed myself in such thoughts, a squeaky voice brought me back to reality. "My confused little sweetie pie, what are you doing sitting there on that bench? Are you trying to hatch an egg? Have you decided to spend the night out here in the park? Don't you see it's getting dark? Come on, cupcake, I wouldn't want you to catch a chill and keep my up all night with your sneezing."

It was already irritating that Lorelai called my 'sweetie pie' and 'darling,' but recently her repertory had expanded to include new and even more ridiculous names, 'cupcake' being one of them.

I followed her without a word. Then as we were going up the stairs, I asked her, "Listen Lorelai, would you be annoyed if we cut to pieces that red blanket on the bed? Or the blue one with white stripes we bought in Morocco?"

As I'd anticipated, she looked at me as if I'd gone crazy, replying, "It's fine with me, but afterwards we should set fire to the Persian rug in the purple parlor."

Lorelai had this gift for letting me know when I'd crossed the line. I suddenly realized that an explanation was necessary. We sat down on the red couch, and as she caressed my hair I brought her up to speed on the latest developments. When I finished the story Lorelai let out a groan, saying, "But seriously, my little teapot, are you really going to believe that kooky old Miss Morty? She told you 'break open the cover,' and you go straight back home to destroy all our blankets!"

"She wasn't the one who said it - it was One-Eyed Buck!"

"One-Eyed Buck, One-Eyed Buck ... this is what you get for trusting a pirate! And it makes no sense at all. Once you've broken open all the covers, what will you have gained?"

I couldn't disagree with her, so I remained silent.

Seeing my frown, Lorelai said to me, "Listen, buttercup. It doesn't make any sense to me but if you really want to do it, at least start with the smaller ones. There's that little pink and green one on the sofa that I've never …"

"What did you say?" I exclaimed, interrupting her.

"I was saying," she said, a bit taken aback by my reaction, "that you could start by ripping up that little cover …"

"Stop right there!" I exclaimed, interrupting her again and jumping to my feet. She jumped to her feet as well, thinking that a killer had appeared at the door or that the house was going up in flames. But I took her in my arms, kissed her and said, "What would I do without you! I've always known you were a genius!"

"But what did I say?"

"You said 'the little cover!' And that's just the cover we have to break open! The cover of One-Eyed Buck's diary! Surely there's something hidden inside."

I took her by the hand and we ran up to the library.

CHAPTER 4

On the way up I grabbed the case with the two Malaysian *kriss* inside and Lorelai's sewing basket, and when we'd reached the library I set about carefully examining One-Eyed Buck's diary.

"I am sorry to have to ruin this beautiful diary. After all, it is a manuscript from 1600," I said, though Lorelai wasn't listening, distracted by my great-great-grandmother Guendalina's cookbook.

I eventually noticed an almost imperceptible bump on the back of the cover and knew that that was the right spot to break in. I covered my nose and mouth with a surgeon's mask and made Lorelai wear one too. She protested at first, saying I was exaggerating as usual, but her objections fell on deaf ears for I was firmly determined to do things right. With the sharp Malaysian dagger, I made a tiny incision on the side of the bump and with a pair of tweezers extracted the piece of paper I found hidden within. We were almost there now. I asked Lorelai to hand me a needle and thread which I used to sew up the cut with stitches, so small and close together that the suture was nearly invisible. All this took me back to the time when during the war of Tarapàz, despite the fact that I'd only studied medicine for a couple of years, I was enrolled as a surgeon in that field hospital at an altitude of six-thousand meters. It was there that I'd become so handy with needle and thread. Lorelai complimented my work as well, and as soon as I took of the mask she gave me a smacking kiss.

The moment had finally come to read the note. The type of paper was identical to the pages in the diary, but too small to contain a map. I opened it to find a short poem which I read aloud while Lorelai listened, lying comfortably on the yellow couch with blue and white flowers. The poem recited:

This shall be your first indication:
the pharaoh's tomb's your destination.
Atop the tallest of sisters three,
among the stars, up there you'll see,
what's concealed beneath a stony face
shall lead you to another place.

I was both disappointed and content at the same time. Disappointed because I'd hoped to find what I was looking for immediately, but content as well because we could continue the hunt.

Lorelai, who'd immediately gotten the gist of

17

things, was the first to comment: "How fun! A treasure hunt with clues!"

I didn't quite share her enthusiasm, but I could nonetheless see the positive side of the matter.

"This will be a great chance for us to take a little trip," I said.

"You read my mind, darling," she chirped. "I'll hurry up and pack."

She disappeared in the blink of an eye and didn't come back for over an hour. When she reappeared downstairs in front of the doorway, her green jacket already on and a little hat on her head, she had with her three small suitcases, two big ones and a trunk that was taller than she was. I looked at her with the expression I generally use for hypnotizing flies and told her that she could bring - at the most - *one* of the smaller bags. A quarter of an hour of negotiating later, we settled on a small suitcase with wheels and a purse. I took only a light backpack for myself.

We quickly caught a cab to the airport. The driver was not however one of those normal cabbies who sit there silently, drive with great skill and get you rapidly to your destination of choice. This guy, on the other hand, was a consummate blabbermouth and what's more, obsessed with the idea that half of Earth's population was composed of aliens disguised as humans, ready to take over the planet. Some people really shouldn't overdo it with science fiction.

I wasn't even listening to him, but Lorelai, on the other hand, was really eating it up and asking him millions of questions. He couldn't believe his luck.

He assured her his information was absolutely reliable since it had been referred to him by his cousin, who'd seen one of these aliens unscrew his arm behind the frozen food case at the supermarket. He explained to her that the aliens could be easily recognized by how they spoke, because they all had "the French 'r'." The most important to thing to know however was how to neutralize them. According to him, all you had to do was take talcum powder, to which they were allergic, and blow it in their face.

After a good half hour of similar nonsense, we finally reached our destination. When it came time to pay, I asked the driver if there were any extra fee we'd incurred in return for all his precious information. Lorelai didn't appreciate my attempt at humor, saying that it had all seemed very interesting to her, that you learned something new every day, and that I was troglodyte who was automatically opposed to anything new.

The last person who'd called me a troglodyte was still wondering exactly what type of meteorite had hit him in the head. But Lorelai was Lorelai, and had a license to rave with impunity. When we got to the check-in desk, however, she realized she'd forgotten her passport.

"Passport?" she asked. "Why? Where are we going?"

"To Egypt."

"To Egypt?" she said, her eyes wide as she fell from the clouds.

"That's right, don't you remember? Beneath a stony face ... the pharaoh's tomb ..."

With the same expression she'd made at the porcelain exhibit when she'd broken the precious statue of Paris fleeing after making his rash judgment, Lorelai grabbed my jacket sleeve and whimpered, "Oh sweetie pie, don't make that face. We haven't even left yet anyway. Nothing's changed ..."

It was true. It didn't change anything. We went out to dinner and then to a movie, lugging our baggage along with us. Our departure was merely postponed until the following morning.

CHAPTER 5

The next day our plane left right on schedule. The flight, however, took longer than planned because of a couple of hijackings which fortunately didn't work out. So it was that between the time difference, daylight savings, moonlight savings, and who knows what other new-fangled monstrosities, when we got to Cairo it was already late at night. We found a taxi and asked to be taken to the Three Camels Hotel that Henry, the homeless man in the park, had suggested to me. And so I learned that, at least as far as hotels were concerned, it was better not to trust the advice of a vagrant who was likely to consider luxurious any living conditions slightly better than a cardboard box. Without going into the details, let's just say that there really were three camels, alongside five goats and twenty or so chickens. Now I dearly love animals, but not to the point of desiring to share my bed with them. I expected Lorelai to feel the same, but she showed she had the soul of an animal and then some, lying on the hay as if it were a mattress and snuggling up with a goat. I too was thus forced to adapt to the situation and I settled in between a camel's humps. Strange as it is to say, we slept like babies. Perhaps old Henry's advice hadn't been so baseless after all.

The next morning I woke up a little before Lorelai, and so had time to get acquainted with the camel that had been my pillow. I discove-red that 'he' was actually a 'she,' quite char-ming and with a wonderful personality. For a while we played hide-and-seek. I hid behind one of the columns in the hotel's sizeable atrium and she had to find me. When she gave up, I gave her a whistle and she came running up as happy as can be and licked me all over the face, a display of friendship I would have willingly done without. As soon as Lorelai awo-ke, we prepared our things, said goodbye to our four-legged friends, and set off toward the exit. As we looked outside the door, however, we were greeted by a scene completely diffe-rent from the one we'd encountered the night before. The streets and alleys, which late at night had seemed completely empty and aban-doned, had been transformed at daybreak into a single, gigantic marketplace full of stands, mats, carpets, food, spices, ceramics, animals and, above all, people. It was like being inside a subway car at rush hour. We stood still in the doorway watching this river of varied humanity as it flowed before us. Men with turbans and long tunics, mysterious veiled women, and noisy children passed ceaselessly back and forth. We didn't know whether or not to throw ourselves into the mix. Then, as she took a small step forward, Lorelai suddenly lost her balance, enough so that she was pulled in by the current and dragged away. After two seconds she'd already disappeared from sight. I threw myself in after her but immediately realized it would be no easy task to make my way in the middle of that throng. If I wanted to go forward the current pulled me back; if I wanted to go one way the current took me the other. It was quite frustrating. After half an hour of being bounced aroun, I'd had enough. I went in the first open door I found. To tell you the truth, it wasn't exactly open, but rather hidden by a heavy black curtain with a strange image on it. I only glanced at it for a moment, but it seemed to be portraying a monkey with a turban on its head and scimitar in its hand, astride a rhinoceros launched at full gallop.

Inside there wasn't much light, and it took my eyes a while to get used to that semi-obscurity, given that outside, though it was still early morning, the sun was already blazing. While initially I could see almost nothing, I could however hear a sort of buzzing. It was similar to that of wasps or, better yet, to the hornets that brought me back to my time as a beekeeper amidst the green meadows of Northern Ireland. When I'd begun that adventurous practice, I was so inexperienced that I thought it was necessary to milk the bees in order to obtain honey – a mistake for which I paid dearly. But that's neither here nor there. As soon as my eyes became accustomed to the half-light, I realized I now found myself in a large room illuminated, so to speak, by no more than seven or eight candles. All around me were bearded men, bundled up in ample tunics and wearing turbans on their heads. They were sitting on the ground on small carpets and chanting something incomprehensible which produced that sort of buzzing I'd heard before. In the middle of the room there was a stone table, perhaps an altar, with the same image engraved on it that I'd seen at the entrance. Now that I had more time to look at it, I realized that the monkey and the rhinoceros were chasing after a winged fish. An image that was interesting symbolically, but whose meaning was unclear.

Meanwhile they kept right on buzzing. I assumed that if I'd ended up in the middle of some strange congregation, there must be a reason for it. Or perhaps not. In any case they were all so concentrated that they didn't even notice me, not until I said, "Hello, please go right ahead. Pretend I'm not even here."

Sometimes I doubt whether I might not be a complete idiot. In a flash they all jumped on me, and after a few moments, I found myself bound, laid out on the stone floor in the middle of the room, and in a position which too all intents and purposes was far from comfortable. I must admit that their lightning-fast move had caught me unprepared. They'd been able to surprise me for the simple fact that I'd underestimated them, imagining them to be a bunch of stiff-jointed twits. I thus received the umpteenth confirmation that first impressions can often be misleading.

CHAPTER 6

The bearded men were standing all around me, staring as if they'd never seen anyone in the habit of shaving.

"I beg your pardon if I interrupted you," I said, with a smile that was less than sincere, "If you untie me now I'll get out of your hair immediately," but I might as well have been talking to a wall. They continued to stare at me without saying a word. The idea that they were a bunch of twits once again began to make headway in my mind.

Suddenly their circle opened, and from the other end of the room I saw approaching a tall, thin man who was not only beardless, but completely bald as well. He was much taller than the others and dressed, or rather undressed, like an ancient Egyptian pharaoh. In front of him he held in both hands a gilded (or was it golden?) bowl. Upon reaching me he lifted it up high, pronouncing some strange words to which he seemed to attach great importance but which to me meant nothing at all. One of the bearded men raised my head and brought the bowl to my lips so I might drink its contents.

In it was a greenish liquid in which several red peas were floating. I'd never seen anything like it. If those buffoons thought I was going to drink that slop they had another thing coming. I immediately let them know I had no intention of cooperating, but a sharpened scimitar pressed against my throat was able to convince me more quickly than any amount of reasoning.

When I found myself in similar situations I usually transformed into the hairy, sharp-toothed monster Grunz, but on days of a new moon this mutation couldn't take place. To my chagrin, I thus was obliged to drink that mysterious brew tasting vaguely of citron juice and swamp mud.

I was about to give them a piece of my mind, and specifically that I'd certainly tasted better in my time, when everything around me suddenly vanished, and a moment later I found myself alone in the middle of the desert. No longer tied up, I rose to my feet and looked around. There was nothing but sand in every direction. What kind of a joke was this? Had they drugged me, taken me away and left me in the middle of the desert? What a ridiculous little prank!

So I set off walking under the blazing sun determined to file a complaint at the Tourism Office, but after half an hour I realized I'd been going in circles and was now back where I'd begun. I didn't despair though, as it wasn't in my nature to do so, and at any rate I'd been in worse situations. Like that time when, after drinking too much Carpados juice, I'd fallen off the *Southern Star* into the frigid waters of the North Pole. Not even then had I lost hope - not even when I'd seen the ship sail away and disappear into the dark of night and felt the jaws of the cold paralyze me like a frozen cod. In fact I'd survived. How, you may ask? Truth be told I don't remember too well. I have only very patchy memories of a splendid ice palace and a gorgeous woman white as snow, who gave orders to polar bears as if they were trained puppies.

But if back then I was about to end up frozen to death, now I risked being roasted under the relentless African sun.

I'd just sat down at the top of a dune to think about what to do, when I saw a point in the distance that was getting larger and larger. It was clear that something was quickly approaching and judging by the great cloud of sand it was kicking up, it must have been something big. When it came close enough, I discovered it was that same turbaned monkey astride a rhinoceros and was chasing after a flying fish - that very same band of strange animals I'd already seen in the image on the tent and again on the stone table.

Though the monkey did not have a very reassuring look on his face and was brandishing a scimitar, this was no time to hesitate.

It might be my only chance of getting out of this mess. I snagged the rhinoceros' tail and hung on for dear life. I was dragged away at the speed of a freight train and remained in that precarious position I don't know how long, travelling across kilometers and kilometers of burning desert. Then, at a certain point the rhinoceros' tail became so hot that I had to let go. I did several somersaults on the sand and stopped just in time to watch the monkey disappear beyond the dunes on his powerful steed. I looked around and saw, to my right, something completely unexpected. The three Great Pyramids of Khufu, Khafre and Menkaure rose imposingly no more than a hundred meters away.

CHAPTER 7

In the meantime however, I had begun to doubt whether all this was actually real, and whether I wasn't having some sort of hallucination thanks to that brew they'd made me drink. Since it has to be said, a monkey riding a rhinoceros and chasing after a flying fish just isn't normal. I decided to conduct an experiment, making a small cut on my finger with the Swiss Army knife I always brought with me. From this there emerged not a single drop of blood. In fact the incision I'd made shaped itself into a little mouth which said, "Destiny's plot continues to unravel. Whether or not it's real, you're where you must be."

So I was right! I was smack in the middle of a waking dream (or were my eyes closed?), brought on by that abominable slop they'd forced me to drink. Most likely I was still lying on the stone table amidst those bearded men who were most certainly having a good laugh at my expense, together with their bald-headed friend dressed up as a pharaoh.

But now that I'd discovered the truth, perhaps I could turn things to my advantage. Conscious of being in a dream, I could probably now do things there would normally be impossible. Moreover there was a chance that the dream wasn't completely a dream, but that it also contained elements of reality. There was nothing left to do but put it to the test. The first thing to be done was to exploit the fact I found myself so close to the pyramids of Giza, the summit of the tallest of which was supposed to conceal the second clue from One-Eyed Buck, hidden under a stone.

Well, it was time to see if I could really control the dream rather than being a mere victim of it. I took off at a run and soared into flight. It was working! In a matter of seconds I reached the top of the Pyramid of Khufu, the tallest of the three. Upon searching under the numerous stone fragments lying everywhere I soon found the message I was looking for. I stuck it in my pocket and quickly returned to Cairo in flight where, plummeting from the sky à la Superman, I recouped Lorelai who was still wandering in the middle of the crowd.

"I knew you'd been keeping something from me," she said smiling as we flew over the roofs of the houses.

I tried to explain to her that this wasn't really me but merely an image of me, inside of a dream that was nevertheless capable of interacting with reality. But it was all a bit over her head. We landed in front of the door to the black tent, inside of which were the bearded men, the pseudo-pharaoh, and probably myself as well, lying on the stone table. I told Lorelai to wait outside, fabricated a knotted club out of thin air, and made my entrance. I'd just begun to deal out a few blows left and right when something strange occurred. I felt myself being sucked away and a moment later, my dream self was reunited to my original self which was still lying there on the stone table, though no longer tied-up. The proximity between my two bodies had probably accelerated the end of the potion's effect. Now the situation was more critical than ever. I'd lost my powers and the bearded men had extracted a scimitar from underneath their tunics and were now advancing slowly but surely toward me. I jumped down from the table, but was then forced to retreat until my back was literally against the wall. To make things worse, Lorelai came in, saying, "My crazy little sweetie pie, I just want you to know that if I stay out there a little while longer, the crowd is going to drag me away again."

Now we both had our backs against the wall, one next to the other. If before the situation had been critical, it was now dramatic to say the least. But as always occurred in such cases, my sixth and seventh senses came to my aid. I don't know how I thought of it. I only know that I gave an incredibly loud whistle to which she couldn't help but respond. It was her all right, the hotel camel with whom I'd played hide-and-seek and whom I'd taught to locate me by following the sound of my whistle. She arrived at a gallop, tearing away in her fury the black tent covering the door and thus finally shedding a little light on that dark room. She came to a halt between us and the bearded men and tried to give me an enormous lick on the face, which I ably dodged. I jumped on her back pulling Lorelai up with me, spurred her on, and we galloped away through those streets full of people who, fortunately for them, were accustomed to sidestepping running camels.

CHAPTER 8

We came to a stop when we'd reached the other side of the city. It was now time to say our goodbyes. Our camel friend maintained a dignified front, but as soon as she turned the corner we heard her crying. But such is life - it's always difficult when friends must part ways. Even Lorelai was saddened.

"What a dear old beast," she said. "If she hadn't been so bulky I'd have gladly taken her home."

"I know some people much smaller than her," I commented, "who take up far more space."

"So true! Your Aunt Casimira for example, despite the fact that she's so tiny ..."

"Let's not name names," I cut short, fearing that by evoking Aunt Casimira we might see her appear before us from one moment to the next.

Luckily the part of the city where we were now wasn't as overcrowded as the one we'd just left. We now found ourselves in a rather large, unpaved and semi-deserted square. In that moment a man with a cart and two veiled women were crossing it. Lorelai sat down on low wall, sighed, and said with a sad face, "We've lost all of our luggage."

"Don't worry," I reassured her. "I still have our money and passports with me."

Having spent much of my life travelling around the world, I knew just what you needed to keep with you when you were far from home. For this reason my travel clothes were always full of secret pockets. Lorelai smiled, got up, gave me a kiss and said, "Well done, my organized little sweetie pie, but now we have to find that message from your pirate ancestor," and then, looking around her, "I wonder if the pyramids are far from here."

I wish I'd had a camera with me to capture the stupefied expression on her face when I showed her the message from One-Eyed Buck I'd taken from the top of the Pyramid of Khufu. She demanded to know how I'd done it, and when I explained it to her she was more amazed than before.

We both sat down on the little wall and read the message together:

Until now you've done quite well,
better than I thought, just swell.
Now you must go searching for
something on the ocean floor
My old ship you must locate
and under a beam investigate

His old ship? Considering that One-Eyed Buck had lived in the 17th century, his ship had been at the bottom of the sea for roughly four hundred years. But that wasn't the biggest problem. Rather, it was the fact that I didn't have the slightest idea where it had sunk. I remembered very well having read in Buck's diary that the ship was called the *Rotten Skull*, but there was no indication as to where it lay. I had already begun to see myself obliged to undertake extenuating research in the historical archives of the major ports of the world, when I saw a small, stick-thin old woman approaching, dressed in rags that were elegant in their own way and strangely without the veil that hid the faces of all the other women. Though I didn't generally approve of the custom of covering up one's face, I couldn't help thinking that, in this case, it wouldn't have necessarily been such a bad thing.

"Salàm," she said looking at us.

"Aleikum salàm," I replied, exhausting in these two words nearly my entire Arabic vocabulary.

Fortunately she continued in our tongue. "Do you want to buy this blue desert lizard's tail?"

As she said this, she pulled an old matchbox out of one of the many folds of her dress, opened it, and displayed its contents: the small blue tail of a reptile, dried out and curled up.

I looked at her speechless; Lorelai did likewise.

Feeling perhaps that some explanation was necessary, the old woman added, "It's the most powerful good luck charm anywhere. I've come to offer it to you because it seems to me you need it."

My diffident nature got the best of me and I waved her away with a quick "No thanks," but Lorelai had other ideas.

"Is it really that lucky?" she asked.

"Here we go again," I thought, "just like with the taxi driver."

"Nothing in the world attracts good luck more than this tail," the old lady assured her.

Lorelai took the matchbox, carefully examined what lay within, and finally exclaimed, "I'll take it!"

There and then I thought I ought to say something along the lines of "How can you be so gullible! Wake up! The world is full of frauds! You can't just believe every whopper that gets thrown your way!" and similar such things. Then I remembered I'd just told her I'd flown to the top of the Pyramid of Khufu and crossed the desert by hanging onto the tail of a rhinoceros ridden by a turbaned monkey. So I decided to hold my tongue. And when I heard the old lady was asking only a few cents for her little blue tail, I thought that maybe I'd been wrong about her, and that maybe it was also wrong of me to let my rationality prevail so often over my instincts when the two conflicted.

As if she'd read my mind, the old lady looked at me with penetrating eyes and said, "Yes indeed, you must listen more to your instincts. I always do. If you also do as I do, you shall always be well guided and you shall proceed with a step that is sure and quick."

She thus made a slight bow with joined hands, turned around and walked away. After three or four steps she tripped on a bottle and fell flat on her face. She then got back up, dusted herself off, and continued on her way without turning around until she disappeared down a side street.

"I guess that now that we have the little blue tail," I said to Lorelai, "our problems are as good as solved."

"Ye of little faith, you'll see that, from here on out, our road will become a downhill slope."

"Just as long as we don't slam into a wall at the bottom of it..."

I regretted this remark almost instantly, for Lorelai replied, "Why do you have to be so mean?"

CHAPTER 9

We reached the port of Alexandria by way of an overcrowded local bus. While I was forced to find space on the roof amidst the luggage and twenty-five other people, Lorelai was invited by a charming, young Egyptian man to sit next to him in one of the best seats. The young beau had with him a cooler full of wonderful, ice-cold drinks, such that while I was cooped up on the roof inhaling sand, Lorelai was down below getting fawned over with every courtesy. When we got off she said to me, smiling, "Well, my sandy little sweetie pie, see how well the little blue tail works?"

"For Pete's sake Lorelai, it was only at the start that I doubted that amulet's power for a moment."

"Are you sure it was just for a moment?"

"Well, all right, maybe also when the old lady fell flat on her face, but now I assure you that I believe in it too!"

"Good cupcake, I'm happy to hear that. Now you'll see that it'll bring you luck too."

I sure hoped it would, given that our search

for the pirate ship didn't have much chance of success. We went in the direction of the port hoping to find a historical archive that conserved some trace of the passage of the *Rotten Skull*.

I had decided not to reveal to anyone that I was a descendent of One-Eyed Buck, fearing that my ancestor had been up to no good in these parts and someone might get it into their head to claim damages.

When we reached the port, we noticed a man who was despairing quite theatrically next to a ship at anchor.

"Look at him," Lorelai said. "He reminds me of you when you discovered that the Picasso you'd found in the trash was a fake."

"I've never found a Picasso in the trash," I replied. "You must have dreamed it up. And what's more, I never despair - you should know that."

"A dream, eh? Maybe you're right, but you were really funny just the same."

This was certainly an odd misunderstanding. But comprehensible, given the fact that dreams sometimes seem so real, and reality so much like a dream.

As we walked past him, the man immediately quit moaning, looked me over from top to bottom and bottom to top, left to right and right to left, and then grabbed me by the collar. He was about to say something to me but he didn't have the chance, because anyone who grabs me by the collar never has time to say much of anything. As I've already mentioned, when someone attacks me I generally turn into the hairy, sharp-toothed monster Grunz. But in this case, the danger was of such modest pro-portions that I merely grabbed him by the col-lar and threw him into the water.

Since he didn't seem at all comfortable in this liquid element, and in order to avoid his sinking to the bottom like a lead ball, I threw him a line so he could climb back up onto the pier. It was then that I realized I might have been a bit too impulsive. For when I took a better look at him, he was certainly not the type of man who you'd expect to attack you down on the waterfront. He was quite thin, in jacket and tie, and had a pair of large, round glasses which he fortunately hadn't lost when he'd taken his little swim.

"Why did you throw me in the water?" he asked me, squeezing out his shirt.

"You grabbed me by the collar," I explained to him.

"Really? Is that so? Well, I'll be damned - I'm so upset I don't even realize what I'm doing. I didn't mean to attack you. I merely wanted to ask you if by chance you happened to be an expert in deep-sea diving."

In truth I was. Recently, I'd even participa-ted with Professor Octopus in salvaging some cases of champagne from the wreck of the *Ti-tanic*, but before telling him so I wanted to know the reason for his asking.

His response stunned both Lorelai and me. "It's true, please excuse me. I haven't even introduced myself. My name is George Pataff, history professor, and I've organized the salvage of an old ship named the *Rotten Skull*. We were supposed to depart this morning, but at the last moment the diver in charge of the operation caught the measles."

Lorelai and I looked at each other and both our minds raced to a certain little tail of a blue desert lizard, inside a half-ruined box of matches.

Naturally I offered my full cooperation, saying that we were both ready to leave immediately, but George asked, looking at Lorelai, "Would she be coming as well?"

"Of course," I replied. "What's the problem?"

"It's not a problem for me, but the crew is made up of sailors from the old school, a bit superstitious, and I doubt they would approve of the presence of a woman on board."

"Don't be ridiculous George," I said, as I kindly pushed him towards the ship's gangway and all three of us climbed aboard.

CHAPTER 10

The crew was composed of five men, each one uglier than the one before. I don't know where George had dug up such a raggedy bunch. You could see from a mile away they had only one thing on their mind - robbing him just as soon as he'd pulled anything even minimally appetizing up from the deep.

Lorelai must have had the same impression because despite the fact that they were scowling at her, she went to go shake hands with each of them, saying, "Nice to meet you. I'm Professor McTresor and I'm the only one capable of guiding you on your journey of discovery. I hope you realize that without me, you're not going to find a darn thing."

With these few words she'd all but eliminated the possibility of being thrown into the sea. During the journey I had the chance to discover that while George was surely an excellent historian, he was also an awful sailor. Indeed, he knew many things about famous people throughout history that no one else did, such as the fact that Cleopatra went to buy groceries every morning by bike, or that Napoleon devised his military strategies during many a game of *Risk*. As a sailor on the other hand, he was pathetic. I figured this out because he held nautical maps upside down and always got confused between stern and bow, starboard and port.

But thanks to my help, we were able to reach the point where One-Eyed Buck's ship supposedly rested. It lay at a depth of roughly one hundred meters, next to a small island of volcanic origin which stuck out all alone in the middle of the ocean.

I put on a diving suit, but before I screwed on the helmet Lorelai insisted I put on a woolen scarf as she said it could be quite damp down there. Naturally I objected at first, but in the end I gave in. Then I jumped into the water. Thanks to the thirty-kilogram weight I was carrying in my hands, I quickly reached the bottom and it didn't take me long to find the old carcass of the *Rotten Skull*. As I've mentioned, George may have been worthless as a sailor, but he was quite the ace as far as historical research was concerned. I located a gash in the side of the ship through which I would have been able to enter, if a rather large octopus hadn't suddenly blocked my way. I thought I recognized in him the same octopus that had given me such trouble during the salvage operation of the champagne from the *Titanic*, but I couldn't be completely sure since all octopi more or less look alike. Just as the other one had, this one got it into his head that he wasn't going to let me in but, expert diver that I am, I knew what to do. As soon as the aggressive cephalopod shot out one of his tentacles toward me, I grabbed the end of it and threw it back at him, making it coil around his head. Then, exploiting his momentary disorientation, I took the end of another tentacle and wound it around his head in the other direction. At which point I took a tentacle on the right and knotted it with one on the left, and with another two I made a nice bow on his head. I intentionally left his last two tentacles free so he could us them to run for his life, thus removing his bulky and inopportune presence.

Finally I could get inside the ship, which despite the passage of time was still largely intact, even if it hadn't been able to avoid covering itself with all those incrustations with which good old Neptune never fails to decorate - and not without a certain style - anything that dallies in his domains for a sufficient period of time.

George had told me to take a look and see if there was anything that deserved to be salvaged in and of itself before bringing up the entire ship. I don't know what he was hoping to find but I didn't see anything of interest, apart from a bucket full of jewels. A bucket full of jewels? Hell, what was a bucket full of jewels doing there? One-Eyed Buck had probably forgotten it in the heat of the moment as the ship was going down. I immediately concluded that as his direct descendent, I was the rightful owner of those jewels, but then I remembered having kept my blood ties with the old pirate a secret, and that if I revealed them now no one was likely to believe me. I decided to bring up the bucket and see what fate had in store for me. At the end of the day, what was a little bucket of antique jewels compared to the fabulous treasure I counted on finding at the end of this trail scattered with strange messages that Lorelai and I were following? I decided not to think about it anymore and proceeded to search for One-Eyed Buck's message hidden behind one of the wooden beams, which was the only real reason I was down there at all. I examined every beam in the ship, or what was left of it anyway, and naturally found the message behind the very last one, in what must have been Buck's cabin. Luckily my ancestor had had the wherewithal to insert the small piece of paper in a well-sealed glass bottle so as to keep it dry. The little bottle, however, was terribly stuck behind the beam and simply refused to come out. Even when I pulled on it with all my strength it wouldn't budge. So off the floor I picked up an iron bar, deformed by rust and covered with marine microorganisms, and delivered such a blow that the beam cracked open and the little bottle popped right into my hands. Unfortunately, that beam must have been fundamental to the structural integrity of the entire ship, which collapsed disastrously all around me and disintegrated in a matter of seconds. While I watched the undersea current carry away the cloud of dust into which glorious *Rotten Skull* had been transformed, I asked myself how George would take the news. I personally didn't consider it to be a great loss, but I understood that the point of view of an historian might be slightly different. I rose toward the surface, holding tightly in one hand the little bottle with the message and in the other the bucket full of jewels. But up on the ship a big surprise – in the sense of awful – was waiting for me.

CHAPTER 11

My first thought was that there had been a mutiny, as George was tied up and the sailors seemed to have taken control of the ship. Of Lorelai there was no trace. While I got out of my diving suit as a butterfly emerges from its cocoon, one of the sailors came toward me and I readied myself for battle. But unexpectedly, the ugly mug gave me his hand to shake, saying, "Relax, we're all agents with Interpol and we've finally caught one of the most notorious thieves of historical artifacts in the world."

"Who, George?"

"That's him. Look at this," he said to me, handing me a piece of paper with George's photo, under which it was written 'Wanted for theft and smuggling of works of art.'

George admitted, "It's true, but these men aren't agents. They're pirates!"

Unbeknownst to us, we'd surrounded ourselves with only the finest company on one side and the other.

"You're not about to believe that crook," the ugly mug said to me, displaying a half-toothless smile. "I see that you found something interesting down there. Please show it to us."

"Give them nothing!" yelled George.

"Shut your mouth or I'll throw you into the sea!" the sailor warned him.

"If I weren't tied up, I'd show you a thing or two!"

"I'd like to see that! It's five against one!"

"I'm worth ten of you!"

"Boom!"

"You took me by surprise before, otherwise ..."

"If you don't shut your mouth I'll cut your nose off!"

Few times had I witnessed a conversation of similar brilliance. Just the same I thought I'd heard enough, so I interjected, asking, "Where's Lorelai?"

"That cow just wouldn't stop yapping," replied the pirate, "so we shut her in the hold. But she might be feeling lonely so it's time you go keep her company." The five pirates threw themselves at me, but I quickly turned in to the hairy, sharp-toothed monster Grunz and an instant later, they'd all been disembarked - or rather catapulted - onto that volcanic island near the ship. To get over the headache that always plagued me after my transformation I hit my head repeatedly against the ship's smokestack, and then proceeded to get Lorelai out of the hold. She was quite annoyed.

"Nice idea you had, leaving me alone on a

ship with a band of crooks. While you were taking a swim and enjoying yourself, I had to
contend with all these troglodytes! I was able
to get a few slaps in here and there, but there
were too many of them. And George turns out
to be a scoundrel as well!"

"I know, I know," I told her, and to calm her
down I showed her the bucket full of jewels.
I'm not sure which sparkled more, the precious
gems or her eyes.

"They're beautiful," she said. "So the treasure was there?"

"Which treasure?" asked George, who was
still tied up. We'd completely forgotten about
him.

"This one," I hurried to say, showing him the
bucket. I didn't want him to know there could
be something else beyond that, but I wasn't
sure he'd be taken in.

Now that I knew who he truly was I saw him
with new eyes. No longer did he appear to me
the erudite and slightly naïve little professor
he'd seemed at the beginning, but rather a
treacherous thief ready to snatch your chair
out from under you. I even began to doubt
whether Cleopatra had ever taken her bike to
get groceries, and whether Napoleon really
was an incorrigible *Risk* player.

Suddenly and completely unexpectedly,
George said, "You think you know who I am,
but you do not. My name is Lor W.G. Krewy-
stoz, where the 'W' stands for Wasestejorl and

'G' for Gugj."

When I saw he had nothing else to add, I asked him, "So?"

"I am an extraterrestrial."

Lorelai and I looked at each other, and then she exclaimed, "I told you the cab driver was right!"

"Now you're not going to believe this guy as well!" I shot back.

"It is not about believing," George - or was it Lor? - affirmed, "I can prove it to you. Touch my nose."

"Why should I?"

"If you touch my nose I can read your mind."

"Oh, fantastic!" exclaimed Lorelai, "Can I touch it?" and without waiting for an answer she placed her finger on his nose. I wanted to tell her not to do it and that it might have been a trick, but she didn't give me the time.

George, or Lor, closed his eyes and said, "You live with him in a big, old house in front of a large public park where a werewolf lurks on nights of a full moon."

"That's incredible!" Lorelai exclaimed.

"I see that you've done your homework," I said.

Without letting himself be distracted by our comments, George - or more likely Lor – continued. "When you two are at home you take turns cooking dinner, but you are not very good at cooking so sometimes you buy something pre-cooked and put it on the table as if you had made it yourself."

"Is that so?" I said, as the corners of Lorelai's mouth slowly began to curl into a frown.

"You two are very close, to the point that I can even read through you some information regarding your companion. Sometimes in the evening he goes down to the cellar, saying he is going to meditate, but in reality ..."

"All right, all right, that's enough" I interrupted. "You've convinced us."

"Just as he was about to say something interesting!" Lorelai protested.

"I crashed on your planet over four hundred years ago and in order to leave, I need a purple stone which I believe to be hidden in that bucket in the middle of all the jewels."

A quick investigation demonstrated the exactness of his words. The purple stone was really there and it was bigger and more luminous than all the others.

"And now what do we do?" I asked him and, given that he was still tied-up, I added, "Let's get you out of those ropes."

"It is not important. Take a hammer and break that stone, here in front of me."

With a just one blow from the hammer, the stone disintegrated and in the process produced a blinding flash of light. When we regained our sight after a few moments, we realized that Lor had disappeared and the bucket of jewels with him. All that remained were the ropes with which he'd been bound. Lorelai and I once again looked at each other amazed. We thus learned to our own detriment that you can most certainly be an extraterrestrial *and* a thief at the same time. But these details quickly faded into the background. For the breaking of the stone had produced in us a strange collateral effect – it had transformed us both into monkies.

CHAPTER 12

We remained in this state for nearly two weeks and I must admit it was great fun. The ship was quite large and became one big playground, though a tropical rainforest would certainly have been more suitable. But it's a well-known fact that the secret in life is knowing how to be content with and enjoy what you have.

When we turned back into our old selves again we were all dirty and ruffled, but we were happy. It must be said that monkeys certainly know how to have a good time.

We'd lost our clothes so the first thing we felt when we reassumed our old appearance was the cold, firstly because we were no longer covered in fur, and secondly because the ship had continued to travel of its own accord and had ended up amidst the ice.

We got dressed and sat still for a time, looking at all that ice in the middle of which the ship was passing.

It took a while before our rational mind regained control, but in the end we went back to being two "civilized" people, and at that point I remembered our treasure hunt and the message I'd found at the bottom of the sea which we still hadn't read.

I took it out of the little bottle and read it together with Lorelai. It said:

Impressive indeed, you've gotten up to here.

Congratulations are in order, I must be sincere.

Now you must go if well I remember,

straight to the North Pole, right to the center.

If you arrive, may your courage not sag,

another clue there you'll most certainly snag.

"Cross your fingers, Lorelai," I said. "Let's hope this is North Pole and not the South Pole."

"You're forgetting about this," she replied, smiling and pulling out the little tail of the blue desert lizard.

Now was the time for that pint-sized good luck charm to work its magic, for night was falling and the temperature with it. I went to look at the thermometer in the ship's cabin and it was already at minus twenty. I recalled that time I'd been locked in the cold store of the Hotel Miramar in Madrid. To be more precise, I'd been locked in there by the hotel's owners, the touchiest people I've ever met. They'd taken offense because I'd found fault with the name of their hotel, seeing as there was absolutely no sea to be seen from any of its windows. Anyway so much the worse for them, since I'd turned into the hairy, sharp-toothed monster Grunz, tore off the great door, and escaped with it into the night.

Now it was different though. I couldn't resolve the situation by mutating since no one was attacking or wronging me in any way.

It was necessary to find a solution as soon as possible because the frigid sea water was solidifying around the ship and we would soon be stuck in the ice. Despite all this, there was some good news, that being that the little tail of the blue desert lizard had done its duty and we really were at the North Pole. I knew so by looking at the stars since I saw that Orion was getting together with Venus, while the newborn Gemini were going to Sagittarius on the Great Chariot pulled by Taurus. Lucky I'd taken that astrology class at the University of Astronomy; this way I knew my way around the night sky quite well. But the cold had us in its fierce grip. Even as we held each other as snug as bugs in a rug, we were unable to produce enough warmth. We were like two popsicles, one next to the other in the freezer. We really had to get moving. I set about searching the ship and discovered that there was a mountain of coal at the bottom of the hold. We took this fuel and piled it up at the bow of the ship under cover.

It was excruciating work, by the end of which we were all warmed up and covered in sweat. But the cold was ever lying in wait, so after having opened up a hole on the bridge to let out the smoke I hurried to light the coal. This was no simple matter, however, as I had no matches or lighter. I no longer carried them on me ever since I quit smoking years before. Then I had smoked like a chimney. I'd developed the habit through the fault of my next-door neighbor, a descendent of the Apaches, with whom I often argued because he was always shooting arrows into my yard. Then every time we buried the hatchet, I had to smoke the peace pipe with him for an entire afternoon. The fact remained that we now had nothing with which to light the coal. However, I managed to do so just the same by evoking the sacred fire of the god Agni with a ritual my Hindu Religion teacher in elementary school had taught me.

The bow of the ship was thus transformed into an enormous oven capable of melting its way through the ice. It was an amazing spectacle to see the front of the ship burning red-hot in the dark of night while the ice melted away and turned to froth the water below. We also took advantage of that heat, falling asleep like two curled-up kittens before a glowing fireplace. We slept soundly as we were exhausted from our monkeying-around and after hauling all that coal. But a rude awakening was in store for us just before dawn. For despite the fact that the ship had been making its way for days without any guidance, it had not yet learned to avoid obstacles and so crashed into an enormous pole sticking out of the polar ice-pack. It was a mammoth pylon with spiraling red and white stripes like a barber-shop sign. It was one hundred meters in diameter and at least five times that tall. I knew immediately what we were dealing with - it was the terrestrial axis around which our planet turns. That meant that we now found ourselves exactly at the center of the North Pole, precisely where One-Eyed Buck had said to go look for his message. We jumped down from the ship as happy as can be and began to walk around that huge pillar until we found what we were looking for. The fourth message in our treasure hunt was attached with a half-rusted nail, as cold and rigid as a frozen sole.

CHAPTER 13

"Quick, take it off!" Lorelai exclaimed, but I stopped her, saying, "Wait, don't touch it! Let's read it first!"

And so, through the veil of ice that covered it, we read:

Here there's no doubt, you'll be freezing cold,
Hawaiian beaches are certainly better, all told
There where reign the most heavenly climes
There lies an old temple that's fallen on bad times
To the god Perepè it is dedicated
And under the altar your message has waited

"What do you think?" I asked Lorelai.

"It's not exactly around the corner, but at least it's warm. My feet are literally frozen."

I tried to detach the message, but it was completely frozen and shattered between my fingers. Lucky we'd read it first.

"Shall we go back to the ship?" Lorelai proposed.

"Yeah, though I'm not sure it'll be able to sail after the blow it's taken."

Having already completed three-quarters of a lap around the pole of Earth's axis, we were proceeding in the same direction in order to get back to where we'd begun. After another twenty steps or so, however, we ran into something unexpected. There was a small door in the pole, complete with doorbell. I rang it, but no one came to answer. I rang it again, but the door remained shut.

"There's nobody there," I said.

"Let me try," said Lorelai. "You're too polite," and she proceeded to press the buzzer uninterruptedly for a good quarter of an hour.

Finally the door opened and a big, burly man with a long, thick black beard appeared in the entryway in his pajamas and slippers.

"Who's ringing so rudely at this time of day?" he exclaimed in his deep, baritone voice. "Is it not possible to get a little peace and quiet even at the Pole?"

"Excuse us," chirped Lorelai, brandishing one of her most captivating smiles, "we hadn't realized it was so early. But our ship is half-sunk, it's cold as hell out here, and we have to get to Hawaii."

If there was one quality Lorelai possessed it was a capacity for synthesis, a synthesis that could be so synthetic, however, as to leave her interlocutor at a loss.

Stupefied, the bearded man asked, "Hawaii?"

"Yes, those beautiful islands in the Pacific Ocean ..."

"I know where Hawaii is!" the man exclaimed and fell silent with a frown, probably trying to get things straightened out in his mind.

"Listen, what do you say you let us in and offer us a hot cup of tea?" Lorelai proposed, further reinforcing her smile and thus bringing it to such brightness as to necessitate the use of sunglasses. The big bearded man's stern armor of cantankerousness began to crack. And rightly so, given that in the preceding months he'd seen nothing but the whiskered snouts of seals and walruses turn up at his door, and faded-white polar bears wander like ghosts up and down the ice-pack. In my opinion, rather than being so ornery, he ought to have jumped for joy at the sight of a beautiful, smiling blond begging him to let her into his home. It's true that he might not have been equally enthusiastic at my presence, but it's a well-known fact that perfection is not of this world. He finally made up his mind and let us in. We thus came into a vast, well-lit, multi-use room, well-furnished and, above all, well-heated. In the middle there was a large table with chairs, at the end an unmade bed and the kitchenette, on the left a large and well-furnished bookcase with a large desk in front of it, and on the right a nice couch, a small table, and two armchairs. I immediately sunk into one of the latter while Lorelai offered to make the tea.

Our host sat down on the other armchair and began looking me over from beneath his thick eyebrows. I couldn't help but notice his striking resemblance to a walrus, with the exception of his beard of course. Lorelai soon appeared with a tray carrying an entire tea set. How she'd managed to find it was a mystery, but I wasn't excessively amazed. One of the features that most characterized her was an ability to get her bearings quickly in an alien environment, as if she were in her own home. She set the tray on the little table, sat down on the couch, and while she was filling the teacups she asked our host, "Just what are you doing here, all by your lonesome?"

"You might have heard of me," he said, as we sipped our hot, aromatic beverages. "My name is Rodric."

"Would you happen to be a professional soccer player? Or is it basketball?" guessed Lorelai, who didn't know much about either soccer or basketball. How she'd managed to imagine that big oaf in the act of netting a goal or a basket was beyond me.

His pride wounded by this lack of recognition, he replied haughtily, "I'm a famous writer and I come here to be able to concentrate without being disturbed."

"Oh, so we've disturbed him, the poor man.

We really are mortified. So what are you writing about, then?"

Maybe it was just my impression, but it seemed as though Lorelai was making fun of him.

"I'm writing the history of ancestor my, the pirate Lame Will, his incredible exploits, and his ongoing struggle with his bitter enemy, One-Eyed Buck, that despicable son of a bull shark.

CHAPTER 14

This was really too much! I'd come all the way to the North Pole to have a stranger insult my ancestor, a member of my family who, while I hadn't known him personally, surely deserved more respect than what the bearded Rodric was showing him. I was about to react as the situation demanded when it occurred to me that, when it came right down to it, bull sharks were actually wonderful creatures and therefore being called 'son of a bull shark' wasn't such a terrible offense after all. So I decided to shrug it off.

Lorelai, however, was curious and asked, "Why all this rivalry?"

"They were both pirates and therefore they were in competition. At times they decided to assault the same ship or planned to kidnap the same noblewoman, so they got in each other's way. What's more, they both fell in love with the same damsel."

"Nothing special there," I commented. "These things are the norm amongst pirates."

"Very true," admitted Rodric. "But the worst

of it happened when that idiot One-Eyed Buck, now an old man, had the bright idea of giving all the plunder he'd amassed throughout the years to a swindler, a certain Countess Elena Freghieri of Arraffarraffa, for the purpose of building a hospice for old, retired pirates."

This was all too true.

"My ancestor, on the other hand, wasn't nearly so witless and buried his treasure on an island in the Antilles as any self-respecting pirate would."

"I'm very happy for you," I remarked. "So now all you have to do is scurry on over there and recover the treasure chest, or whatever it is."

"This was in fact my intention," said Rodric, gritting his teeth, "until I discovered while reading my ancestor's diary that One-Eyed Buck, having realized he'd lost all his loot, secretly followed Lame Will, dug up his treasure, and took it for himself."

A moment of silence followed. Then I asked, "Do you have proof?"

"What?"

"There's no proof. You naturally take as Gospel truth everything your ancestor recounts, but in any respectable court such a grave accusation would have to be supported by the most conclusive evidence."

"Are you a lawyer?"

I responded that I wasn't, even though on the Boga Boga Islands I had successfully de-

fended the young Luana, accused of having se-
duced the chief's son with magical arts, in front
of the witch doctor and tribal court.

"No, I'm not a lawyer. But that doesn't pre-
vent me from using my reason. Let's proceed
in an orderly fashion. Your ancestor claims that
One-Eyed Buck pilfered his treasure, correct?"

"Of course!"

"Well, just how had Lame Will accumulated
this treasure? Had he earned it honestly with
the sweat of his brow? Obviously not. He himself had stolen it from someone else. Therefore
I don't see what the problem is. Have you ever
played the card-game Snap? During the game,
you can steal the deck from anyone you want.
But if at the end of the game, even on the very
last move, someone steals yours, there isn't
much you can complain about. Those are the
rules of the game."

With this pitch-perfect reasoning I'd most
certainly displeased Rodric, but I'd garnered
Lorelai's admiration, as she loved to hear me
construct such shrewd arguments.

"I see that you're taking the side of One-
Eyed Buck," said Rodric, "and I wonder why.
I'm beginning to suspect you have some per-
sonal interest in the matter. You two still ha-
ven't told me what you were doing out there.
Have you perhaps come to spy on me?"

"My dear Rodric," I replied, "to think, completely erroneously as you do, that you're
being spied on is certainly not a good sign. Evi-

dently being out here all alone for too long is not doing your mental equilibrium any good whatsoever. But worry not - if they're diagnosed early on these forms of persecution complex can be easily cured. It's obvious that my argument was purely philosophical. As far as I'm concerned, I'd be thrilled if you could find your treasure and go spend it on ice cream, popsicles or whatever else you want. But given what you've told us, that unfortunately seems quite unlikely."

"You still haven't told me what you were doing out there," Rodric insisted.

Lorelai broke in: "Do you really want to know? We're two newlyweds on our honeymoon. We rented a ship, but then a lightning bolt hit our compass, the captain abandoned us, a whale broke our rudder, we fell asleep, and here we are! And now that everything's been cleared up, would you mind if we put on a little music?"

Lorelai was like this. She couldn't stand boring people, and she was fed up with Rodric and all his questions. When she found herself in these situations she felt as if she were suffocating. So she would invent something to extract herself as quickly as possible, anything that would allow her to get some fresh air, without bothering to think if the solution she'd come up with was logical or not.

As was to be expected, her response gave little satisfaction to the bearded writer, who asked, "Do you take me for a fool?"

I could think of nothing better than to continue along my previous line of argument. "Here we see again your ridiculous persecution complex. The problem is that whatever we tell you, for example that we were out there getting some fresh air, that we'd gotten lost during an office outing, or that we'd come to ski in the area and were waiting for the bus to return home, you would never believe it. Your nebulous mind leads you to see enemies and threats wherever you look."

For a moment I feared that I'd exaggerated with that 'nebulous' and that this time Rodric would truly get angry, but fortunately he kept his calm. Though he looked the quarrelsome type, he showed he knew how to resist provocations. The prolonged solitude of his voluntary retreat, contrary to what I was trying to persuade him, had probably had a positive influence on his character.

"Actually, dear sir," he replied, "you couldn't be more wrong."

It always felt strange to be called 'dear sir.'

"If you had told me you were waiting for the bus I would've believed you, since it stops every morning right outside the door. In fact, I believe it's passing by as we speak."

Lorelai and I looked at each other, most rudely got up and ran outside without so much as a goodbye, and were just able to catch this unexpected means of public transport that was already closing its doors, ready to depart.

CHAPTER 15

This bus wasn't like the ones we were used to. It was longer and jointed, like a small train, and ran on tracks instead of wheels. Contrary to what you might have expected in that region, it was quite crowded with hooded men and women dressed in fur coats. At first glance they looked like Eskimos and, in fact, they were. We realized as much at future stops, seeing that the bus picked them up as it wove between their igloos. The strange thing was that people continued to get on but no one ever got off. We asked for an explanation and were told that the bus brought workers to the big factory in Fridgepot. This was certainly no problem for us, since from there we would certainly find some means of continuing our voyage.

Fortunately it wasn't cold inside the bus so the trip was quite pleasant, apart from some quick turns the driver was forced to execute every now and then to avoid seals or walruses. These were maneuvers to which the other passengers were accustomed, but which several times sent us newcomers falling flat on our backs. For the most part, however, the trip went quietly and smoothly across the white polar landscape.

We were silent for a while. Then Lorelai said, "What a coincidence running into the house of great-grandson of the very pirate your ancestor stole the treasure from."

I didn't respond, for I was intent on looking out the window at a pair of polar bears running alongside the bus much as dogs do where we come from. At least these didn't bark.

"Rodric wasn't very nice, was he?" continued Lorelai, but I didn't hear her this time either, because I was watching with curiosity as a boy and girl Eskimo kissed each other the Eskimo way, that is, by rubbing noses. I was thinking that perhaps they did so to warm each other up.

"He was so suspicious!" she continued, "and his conversation was so boring, what a drag, don't you think, sweetie pie?"

But I was still distracted, observing a piece of glacier split off from the side of the ice-pack in the distance.

So Lorelai lost patience, turned away from me, and said, "It was boring all right, but still better than yours!"

"Than my what?" I asked her, but she refused to speak to me for the rest of the trip. Finally the bus reached its destination, passed through the factory gates, and pulled to a stop in the large interior square. All the passengers got off and set off towards their own particular places of work. We were the only ones who remained on board, still sitting in our seats.

"We should get moving," I suggested, but suddenly five security guards with dogs and guns drawn burst onto the bus and ordered us to get off.

I tried to tell them that this was just what we were about to do but they ordered me to be silent. My blood was already starting to boil, though not enough to transform me into the hairy, sharp-toothed monster Grunz. We weren't far away, though, and I let out brief but significant growl in the direction of the dogs. They immediately changed their tune, backing away frightened with their tails between their legs. The guards escorted us up to the fifth floor of the tallest building and took us directly into the office of the factory owner. From the plate hanging outside the door, we learned that this was a certain Philippe Crapòn, evidently a Frenchman.

His office really was over the top - at least twice as big as Rodric's great room - with nice carpets on the ground, nice paintings on the wall, nice furniture, nice armchairs, nice couches, and a large window the size of an entire wall from which you could admire the breathtaking panorama.

"And just who might you be, terrorists? Agitators? Spies?" he asked, standing up from his desk and coming towards us - not out of courtesy, but merely to have a better look at us. "How pathetic to think you could get inside on the workers' bus!"

"You live up to your name, Crapòn," I replied. "I'm not sure how you manage to run this dump if you can't tell your friends from your enemies."

"And so you would be my friends," he said, eying me with his ironic little smile.

"I didn't say that and it's of no importance to me. It was just a manner of speech, but I see that with you I'll have to explain everything. Don't you think that if we'd wanted to disguise ourselves among the workers, we would have dressed like them and gotten off the bus with them? You don't have to be Sherlock Holmes to figure that out. And don't you also think as that it would be better to get rid of that ridiculous goatee?"

Philippe Crapòn remained speechless for moment, and then asked, "Does it look that bad?"

Lorelai broke in: "Don't listen to him. If you want a woman's opinion it looks very nice. But if I were you I'd grow out a moustache as well, à la D'Artagnan."

"À la D'Artagnan, you say?" he asked, stopping for a moment to meditate on that unexpected suggestion, and then added, "Just who then might you two be?"

"Two people certainly much more polite than

yourself," Lorelai shot back at him, "who would never greet two tourists with such rudeness. But maybe the blame lies with the cold here at the North Pole which makes everyone so ill-mannered and suspicious."

With these few, well-chosen words, she managed to tame the arrogant Frenchman almost completely.

"Two tourists, then," said Philippe Crapòn, who still nurtured a small shred of doubt, "And how did you get here?"

"On a ship which, however, has now sunk," I replied.

"And you two are the only ones who have survived?"

"The fact is," Lorelai explained to him, "that George was really an extraterrestrial, so when we broke the purple stone we were transformed into two little monkeys. Then when we got back to normal, we were completely naked so we turned the ship into a sort of giant stove that melted the ice, but we fell asleep and the ship crashed into the terrestrial axis and sank."

I had refrained from sharing all these details so as not to put our credibility at risk, but once again Lorelai's candid sincerity obtained a better result than any stratagem. After a moment of silence, Philippe Crapòn started to laugh and exclaimed, "Why not, I want to believe you! You really are wonderful people. I do not have visitors very often. Would you like to tour the factory?"

"Sure," replied Lorelai, smiling.

As we descended in the elevator, I asked, "What do you produce here?"

"What else *could* we produce at the North Pole?" Crapòn responded. "Ice cubes!"

CHAPTER 16

It's incredible how some people have such a knack for business that they can see a chance for profit just about anywhere. To me those evocative polar landscapes were simply an incredible panorama to be admired in silence, and it would never have occurred to me to smash those beautiful, candid, sparkling mountains for the purpose of turning them into so many little cubes of ice. This idea had however occurred to Monsieur Crapòn, who proudly showed us how his workers sliced them once and then sliced them again, first one way and then the other. Halfway through our tour he asked me, "Would you like to stay here and work for me? I just happen to need someone I can trust to direct the Counting Department."

"Counting what?" I asked.

"Ice cubes, naturally."

True, it was a stupid question.

I wondered how it had come to him to make me such a chilling proposal, in every sense of the word. I couldn't understand just how he might consider me someone to be trusted. For all he knew, I could have murdered his grand-mother the previous week. I thought he must have been at the Pole for a bit too long and that his brain had frozen. I thanked him, but declined the offer.

Crapòn then brought us to see the heliport. It was from here that the little cubes of ice departed, to be transported all over the world. There was a constant traffic of helicopters taking off full of their frigid merchandise, and then returning empty to be filled up once more.

I immediately glimpsed the chance to bum a ride, but Lorelai was even quicker. "Is there one that's going to Hawaii?" she asked. "Could you give us a ride down there?"

"You are in luck," replied Crapòn. "The helicopters are usually full to the brim with ice and there is no space for passengers, but the load for Hawaii is composed of one single cube, so there is plenty of room."

"A single cube?" I said amazed.

"Yes. It is for an American billionaire who has it brought to him every day to chill his whiskey. Truth be told, it costs him a pretty penny. But he can afford it."

"Honey," Lorelai asked me with her most charming little voice, "when we get back home, can we have an ice cube brought to us from the North Pole?"

I thought she'd said this just to impress Monsieur Crapòn and make him believe that we were rolling in money as well, but then I saw from her expression that she'd been serious. It wasn't the first time this had happened, her desires leaving her mouth an instant before being filtered through her brain. So I suggested to her: "Put a couple of them in your pocket. That way, we don't have to have them delivered."

Shrewd businessman that he was, Crapòn asked to be paid for this passage to Hawaii, but I told him that Lorelai was a famous makeup artist of famous actresses and actors and that the advice she'd given him about growing a moustache à la D'Artagnan was worth far more than our trip in the helicopter. I saw his nose begin to wrinkle, so I also promised him that I'd mention his ice to my cousin Oscar, director of an important popsicle factory in Southeast Asia.

Just as with a painter you generally talk about paintings and with a musician about music, in order to arouse the interest of a businessman you must always be proposing him some attractive opportunity for making money.

Finally convinced, Philippe Crapòn gave us his blessing and we climed aboard the helicopter which was almost completely empty, given that its cargo consisted in a single little cub of ice stored in a small refrigerator.

Once we'd departed, Lorelai said, "The Pole sure is beautiful, but a bit too cold for my liking." "You can say that again, Miss," responded unexpectedly the helicopter's pilot, a dark-skinned man. "I used to live on the equator, and I suffered so much from the heat that I decided to move northwards. But I may have overdone it."

"I'd say so," replied Lorelai. "Can't get much further north ..."

"My cousin Amos did something similar," I said, "when after having risked dying of thirst in the desert, he returned home and drank so much that he drowned."

"Why, didn't he know how to swim?" asked the pilot, at which point I decided the conversation could just as well end there.

When we landed in Hawaii, we were festively greeted by beautiful girls and strapping young men in their traditional costumes. They put flower leas around our necks while playing the ukulele and dancing the hula, their traditional dance in which Lorelai immediately joined. Next there followed a banquet in which our pilot participated as well. What an extraordinary welcome! Extraordinary, right up to the point when our hosts told us that one of us would have to take part in the walk across incandescent lava, a wonderful little ritual they'd probably conceived to communicate to new arrivals the full extent of the warmth of their hospitality. As soon as he heard about this requirement, our friendly pilot suddenly felt an overwhelming nostalgia for the icy Pole. He thanked everyone, said goodbye and flew away like a dragonfly trying to escape a hungry toad. We were thus the only two left, and I certainly couldn't ask Lorelai to put her dainty, Cinderella-like feet at risk. But then I already had a plan in mind.

We walked in procession to the place where our Hawaiian friends had prepared "lava lane" and the whole way we were kept separated, as I had to stay with the little group of candidates for the ritual stroll. Not for a moment did Lorelai cease to shoot me worried looks, to which I tried to respond with gestures as reassuring as possible. When we reached our destination, I sat down off to the side, took off my shoes, and told the others to go right ahead and start without me as I first had to massage my lower extremities to prepare them for the harsh trial that awaited them. But in reality I was secretly rubbing the soles of my feet with the little ice cube the helicopter pilot had entrusted to me in a special little thermos, after having entreated me to deliver it to the American billionaire. I rubbed the cube until it had melted completely and then I did my little walk over the burning lava, which could do no more than warm my semi-frozen feet most pleasantly. Everyone congratulated me, and even Lorelai was very proud of me. She gave me a smacking kiss, saying I'd been great and that when we returned home, I absolutely had to give a repeat performance. After this umpteenth stunt of mine, I located an ice cube from some random

refrigerator, got directions to the American billionaire's villa, and set off in that direction with
Lorelai, but only after having thanked and said
a proper goodbye to everyone, naturally.

CHAPTER 17

I'd never seen such a villa. It must have had a hundred rooms and seemed to have been designed by an architect who'd received his degree in a loony bin. Stylistically it was a mix between a spaceship, a condo complex, an aircraft carrier, and a mall. In a word, it was awful, a pure and simple ostentation of wealth devoid of any good taste which completely disfigured the surrounding landscape.

Lorelai didn't want to step foot in there and told me, "You go. I'll wait for you on the beach," but she didn't have the time to escape. The owner of that monstrosity came out the front door and rode toward us on a motorized kids' scooter, along the asphalt driveway that snaked its way through the well-cured lawn in front of the villa.

He was overweight and wore a straw hat, sun glasses, a loose and colorful short-sleeve shirt, khaki shorts and a pair of loafers with white socks. As soon as he got to us, he hopped off his little toy and offered his hand, saying, "Dear prince, dear princess, welcome to my humble abode. I'm Henry Bigmoney. You're late, the party's already started. Was there a problem during your trip?"

Prince? Princess? I imagined he was a typical exemplar of the newly rich who wanted to make his entrance into the world of the aristocracy, and thus threw sumptuous parties to which he invited any noble - genuine or otherwise - he could get his hands on.

"There must be a mistake," I replied. "We've only come to bring you an ice cube …"

"My husband the prince," interrupted Lorelai, "meant to say that we were delayed because, before coming here, we stopped off at the North Pole to freshen up our outlook on life, and there we met Monsieur Crapòn, who asked us the favor of bringing you your ice cube. We apologize for the delay."

Both the billionaire and I, each for his own reasons, were left agape by this explanation of hers. Then the American said, "Your husband? But isn't Prince Vladimir your brother?"

It's true what they say that lying doesn't pay.

Yet Lorelai didn't even flinch. "My brother Vladimir had to say in Moscow so he couldn't come. So my husband, Prince Popoff, came in his place."

'Prince Popoff?' If she had to make up a name for me, she could at least have found one less ridiculous.

Lorelai decided it was better to cut things

short, asking impatiently, "So are we going to go to this party, or do we have to stay out here all night? And you, Poppy, come on, give the man his ice cube."

So now I was Poppy! I might as well have been a dog. Yet I knew all too well what had just happened. As soon as Lorelai had heard talk of a party, she'd immediately assumed there'd be dancing, and thus hadn't hesitated for a moment to conjure up some tall tale to get herself inside.

I delivered the ice cube to the billionaire who thanked me, saying, "Thanks, but you didn't need to go to all this trouble. And now please, Princess Irina, Prince Popoff, if you'd like to climb on board my scooter ..."

"No thank you. You go on ahead," I responded. "We'll walk."

The corpulent American got back on his little contraption and coasted back toward his horrible villa, and when he got there, he stopped to wait for us at the entrance. I thus had time to exchange a few words with Lorelai.

"Would you like to tell me what's gotten into you?"

"Sorry, my honest little sweetie pie, but how could we miss out on such an opportunity?"

This may have been true, but I would've willingly missed out on it because, unlike Lorelai, I had no great love for parties. But now I was Prince Popoff, a.k.a. Poppy, and there was no getting out of it.

I sometimes got to thinking that without Lorelai, my life would have been much simpler - but probably much more boring as well.

We entered the villa and passed all the way through it from one end to the other as the party was outside in the back. We thus went through an infinite series of rooms of all sizes until we emerged into the vast garden where, as I'd imagined, our billionaire friend had gathered a sizeable herd of representatives from the noble class. Not that they had 'noble' written on their foreheads, but it was all too visible from their clothes, jewels, uniforms, medals and particularly from the snobby airs and arrogant attitude of the guests. Despite the fact that we'd been introduced as Princess Irina and Prince Popoff, we too were looked down on because of our less-than-aristocratic attire. Some of the other guests even went as far as casting doubt on our titles, interrogating us, "What is your house?"

As usual, Lorelai promptly replied, "We belong to the minor branch of the family of Tsar Nicholas II. We directly descend from good old Nicky's mother-in-law's cousin's nephew."

A smokescreen, as usual. Sometimes I suspected that little blond had taken lessons in mimetics from some ink-shooting octopus.

The funny thing was that despite numbering pirates, brigands and politicians – persons, that is, of the worst sort – among my ancestors, I did however have one forebear who in the 14th

85

or 15th century had earned the title of Viscount of Catsinapples by rescuing the king's cat from a tree - an apple tree to be precise.

Yet the one who was really in trouble was Mr. Bigmoney, the host. Despite doing all he could to entertain his guests, he was unable to break down that wall of frigid disdain which surrounded the world to which he desperately wanted to belong. It really is true that we sometimes waste our time and energy to obtain things of little or no worth.

What's more, the poor billionaire didn't have the slightest idea of how to go about achieving his goal. He'd brought over a cowboy band from Texas to play country music and organized a series of games - a sack race, horseshoe toss, and the spanking game – that certainly could not satisfy the refined tastes of people accustomed to frequenting the world's most distinguished courts, and who'd learned to waltz before they could walk.

Nor was the food and drink displayed on the tables very appropriate; hamburgers, French fries, popcorn and Coca-Cola were certainly not the type of fodder to offer people bred on caviar and champagne.

Even Lorelai, whose only nobility was that of the heart, had been disappointed by a party in which she'd hoped to have the chance to dance her socks off.

While on the one hand it was irritating to see Mr. Bigmoney so mistreated by that bunch of snobbish asses, on the other I couldn't help but see the comic side of the situation he'd gotten himself into. Lorelai however truly felt sorry for him, seeing the poor billionaire's clumsy attempts at social climbing. When she saw him go off alone and sit sadly on a bench next to his lake of swans, she went to sit down beside him. It was at times like this that her nobility of heart - the only nobility that really matters - always shone through.

I suddenly realized how hungry I was, so I went to rustle up an abundant ration of French fries and popcorn. As I was peacefully nibbling, I noted a certain movement among the ranks of the nobles of the male sex. Having abandoned their dames, they'd gathered together in a small hut and begun to talk amongst themselves. Every once in a while, they peered out at the bench where Mr. Bigmoney and Lorelai were seated and cackled like a band of off-duty hyenas. These so-called nobles, forgetting the ancient rules of chivalry to which the founders of their houses had sworn loyalty, had decided to play a dirty trick on their host and so demonstrate the full extent of the scorn they nurtured for anyone not a member their caste. Their biggest mistake, however, was to include Lorelai and myself in their treacherous scheming.

It all happened very quickly. I saw a squad of gentlemen take off in the direction of Mr. Bigmoney and Lorelai, and simultaneously I felt myself grabbed from behind and pushed forward by a dozen or so hands. A few seconds later, all three of us - Mr. Bigmoney, Lorelai and me - were all soaking with the swans in the miniature lake.

Now, maybe for these inexperienced noble heirs this was supposed to be a mere prank, something to laugh about in the future when it was brought up at one of their clubs or at some dinner among friends. But there was a minor detail they hadn't taken into consideration. Within an instant, I turned into the hairy, sharp-toothed monster Grunz and was upon them with an impressive leap. At which point there ensued a general stampede - dukes running here, countesses fleeing there, lords retreating upstairs, ladies escaping downstairs, until the battle was finally over and Lorelai, Mr. Bigmoney, and I could finally enjoy the rest of the evening in peace. Apart, as always, from the headache which afflicted me after transforming into the monster Grunz, but for which, as usual, I found some quick relief by banging my head against the wall.

CHAPTER 18

Grateful to us for having freed him from that "despicable rabble" (or so he now called all those belonging to the nobility, us two excluded of course), Mr.Bigmoney invited us to stay with him as his guests for a few days and we accepted most willingly. This way we'd be able to devote ourselves with the necessary tranquility to our search for the temple of the god Perepè, the only real reason we'd come to Hawaii.

Though the American billionaire - who we later learned had made his money producing headwear in the shape of bunny ears and pens with whistles - no longer aspired to noble titles or other such nonsense, Lorelai made up her mind just the same to make him a little more presentable. I protested, saying that it was a hopeless enterprise whose only result would be to waste our time, but she explained to me: "My hasty little sweetie pie, don't misunderstand me. I just want to give him some advice." So the following morning she went into the city with him, and when they returned an hour or so later, Mr. Bigmoney had been transformed so completely that he seemed a new man. The reason was clearly to be found in his extremely elegant new suit.

Lorelai was in seventh heaven, rightly proud of her work. She came up to me and whispered in my ear, "They say the habit doesn't make the monk, but it's also true that a monk will never dress up as a corporal - even if you beg him to in Chinese."

Why you would want to beg a monk to dress up as a corporal, and in Chinese no less, was a mystery to me. I wasn't always able to understand Lorelai's logic, but I'd also learned that in such cases it was better not to ask for explanations. In any case, Mr. Bigmoney seemed very satisfied, which was a sign that the little blond fairy had once again hit the mark. I was happy too; this bizarre idea of Lorelai's to play Pygmalion to our billionaire had been limited to a simple change of clothes. Now we could finally dedicate ourselves to the search.

For several days we explored the various islands of the archipelago, but without success.

One evening we were sitting on the beach watching the sun plunge into the ocean, and I said, "There's no trace of any temple dedicated to the god Perepè."

"Maybe we're not remembering correctly, and his name's not Perepè," said Lorelai, drawing a flower in the sand with her finger. "Do you remember what was written on that piece of paper?"

"Of course. 'There where reign the most heavenly climes / There lies an old temple fallen on bad times / To the god Perepè it is dedicated / And under the altar your message has waited.'"

Fortunately I had an exceptional memory, acquired perhaps from the elephants in those two years I'd lived among them while studying their behavior.

Lorelai pulled from her pocket the little tail of the blue desert lizard which she still kept inside the matchbox, and shut her eyes almost completely, chanting, "Little tail little tail, do what you were meant to do."

I smiled instinctively. But I also remembered that that strange good-luck charm had already shown its power and deserved the utmost respect.

We began to look around expecting something to happen. We hoped to see someone appear, ready to offer us the clue we needed on a silver platter, but the beach remained completely deserted. Perhaps we were asking too much of that little blue tail. Or perhaps we were committing the usual mistake of waiting for a certain type of luck and ignoring what was there before our eyes. The freezing Pole was now thousands of kilometers away and we were alone at sunset on a marvelous Hawaiian beach, an ocean of crystal-clear water at our feet. Everything was perfect, also because Lorelai had lost her make-up case and so this time I wouldn't be forced to ingest several kilos of lipstick. My lips slowly approached hers while hers approached mine. I wrapped my arm around her and she embraced me as well. Then we slowly sunk into the tepid sand and began to roll around in a dance as old as the world. But wouldn't you know it, after only a couple of rolls a cough coming from behind us interrupted our little tango. We sat up, and as we looked around, we realized that four or five hundred people had appeared from out of nowhere and were now surrounding us. They didn't look hostile - indeed, far from it. They were pleasant and smiling, though in all honesty, I would've preferred meeting them in a better moment.

"Where did they pop out from?" Lorelai asked me in a whisper as we got to our feet and dusted the sand off of ourselves.

"I have no idea," I replied. "Maybe it was the little blue tail that brought them."

An elderly man came forward, tanned like all the others and wearing a light-blue tunic whose edges were woven with gold.

"We apologize if we've disrupted your Nau-Nau ritual."

"Don't worry about it," Lorelai replied. "Our Nau-Nau ritual is only postponed. It's our fault as well. We didn't see you coming."

The old man smiled and said, "Once every

ten years we gather here to celebrate the great ceremony in the temple."

"Once every ten years?" whispered Lorelai. "And it had to be just at this very instant."

Then I asked the old man, "What ceremony? What temple?"

"It's a very important ceremony whose purpose is to awaken nature, which would otherwise fall asleep and thus precipitate the world into chaos."

"How wonderful!" exclaimed Lorelai with her usual enthusiasm. "So it's a sort of universal alarm clock. And just how do you perform this awakening? Do you play trumpets or something like that?"

"We don't do it directly. The god Perepè does. The ceremony takes place in his temple."

Lorelai and I looked at each other. Then I whispered to her, "Make sure you don't lose that little blue tail. It really is a life-saver."

"Why should I ever lose it?" she replied, as if I'd said the most ridiculous thing in the world. She then took the Hawaiian in the light-blue tunic by the arm and said to him, "Well, what are we waiting for? Let's go give sleepy old nature a wake-up call!"

CHAPTER 19

So off we went. The man we'd spoken with was named Babo, and he must have been a sort of priest or chief because he walked in front of all the others. Both the men and the women walked in a strange manner, rhythmically stamping there feet into the ground in an Indian-style dance that Lorelai wasn't long in joining.

"How come you stamp your feet so much?" I asked.

"We're already starting to give nature a good waking-up. The vibrations reach all the way to the center of the Earth, where the god Perepè dwells. This way he knows we're on our way to his temple."

All things considered, it was a quite logical explanation.

Stamping away, we entered into the forest that extended for kilometers behind the beach. Soon after we reached a clearing, in the middle of which there rose a stone shrine, very nice despite its having seen better days. It was very small, however, able to hold no more than about twenty people. Unconcerned by this, Babo began to let people in and Lorelai and I watched in amazement as four or five hundred people made their entrance into the shrine without the slightest problem.

"How is it possible?" I asked.

"This is only possible once every ten years," Babo replied. "It's a sign that Perepè has heard us coming and is beginning to perform his wonders."

We entered as well and were left speechless. The interior of the temple was incredibly vast; it seemed as though we were inside a cathedral large enough to contain easily two or three times this many people. The vaulted ceilings, walls and columns were all decorated with naturalistic-style figures and in the center there was the altar, covered by a red sheet upon which sat a gilded (or was it golden?) trumpet. According to One-Eyed Buck's instructions, our message was to be under that altar. The problem, however, was how to go about collecting it under the gaze of five hundred people.

Without my having asked him anything, Babo said to me, "Here inside the temple we are in another dimension, far more ethereal and less solid than normal."

"What do you mean?"

"To give you an example, it's possible to teleport yourself from here to any other place by merely thinking about it."

"Can I try?"

"Of course. But don't think of a place that's too far away, as you might not be able to come back." A moment later I was already underneath the altar, where no one could see me thanks to the long, red cloth that covered it. I searched everywhere and soon found the message, folded up and stuck in a crack. I took it, opened it up, and even if there wasn't much light, I read it. This was what was written:

Now that the whole world you've certainly gone 'round
To be grateful to me for this trip you are bound.
Now to make your return the moment has come
Even if you've found nothing, not the least sum.
But still there is something that you do not see.
When in your home once again you will be
If in the evening your sleep's slow in coming
Look for the blackcap and hear what he's saying

Why that old rascal! So the great treasure hunt ended there, with a message telling me to go back home and start listening to little birds chirp. If One-Eyed Buck thought this was all very amusing he was dead wrong. On the other hand, I too was partly to blame – I should never have trusted a pirate. I stuck the message in my pocket and teleported myself back next to Lorelai and Babo. I was about to tell Lorelai about the message and that at this point we might as well take off, when suddenly the light in the temple dimmed and we found ourselves immersed in a pleasant half-light, like at the theater just before the beginning of the show. I decided to wait for the end of the ceremony. After several minutes the light began to dim even further, and the more it did so the more the golden trumpet sitting atop the altar began to glow, until it remained the only thing visible in an otherwise total darkness. Lorelai whispered in my ear, "Babo explained to me that it won't be long before the god Perepè chooses the purest, most candid soul among those present in the shrine and then, acting through him or her, will proceed to sound the trumpet."

"But why all this darkness?"

"The darkness serves to conceal the identity of the trumpeter."

Slowly, everyone began to sing. It was a strange chant that began slow and monotonous but then became faster and gained rhythm until it became almost reggae-like, though even more enthralling.

Suddenly the trumpet rose from the altar. Because of the darkness, it seemed as though it had risen up of its own accord, but in reality someone had taken it and was beginning to play. Its blast joined the chant to produce a most exquisite music. I'd never heard such sound, such rhythm, such a trumpeter. I'm no great fan of dancing, but that time, moved by an irresistible force, I threw myself uncontrollably in with the others. There were many of us and it was pitch black, but despite dancing as freely as could be, no one ever collided with anyone else. I felt within me a new energy, fresh and clean. That trumpet's blast truly was waking nature from its slumber.

I don't know how long we continued dancing to the sound of that trumpet. No one felt the least bit tired. And what lungs that trumpeter had! Then the music ended with a haunting solo, the trumpet was once again placed upon the altar, and we all found ourselves, I'm not exactly sure how, in the exact same position we'd been in at the beginning.

The light slowly returned and when it had done so, Babo said to us, "This is the first time strangers have participated in this ceremony. I hope you've enjoyed it."

"Can we do it again?" asked Lorelai.

Babo started to laugh and replied, "Most certainly, in ten years' time. Now, however, we must leave before the shrine returns to being as small inside as it is outside. The magic is wearing off, but it will still last long enough to allow us to get out."

"Then the teleportation will also stop working," I said.

"Yes."

"Then, dear Babo, we really must be going. Thanks for everything."

I warmly shook his hand, then grabbed Lorelai and told her to think intensely of the park in front of our house. A moment later we were already there, sitting on a bench and still wrapped up in our embrace like two lovebirds.

"What happened?" Lorelai asked, looking around her incredulously.

"We're home. We teleported back."

"Oh" was all she could say. She still seemed a bit shaken from the ceremony. I, on the other hand, was really feeling great, full of energy. I made to give her a kiss but she pulled back, putting a hand in front of her mouth.

"Is everything all right?" I asked her.

"Great," she replied. "But my lips are still hurting after having played that trumpet for so long."

CHAPTER 20

"And our treasure hunt?" asked Lorelai. "We left without picking up the message."

"I've got it," I replied, taking it out of my pocket and handing it to her.

From the expression on my face, she knew right away that something was amiss. She read it carefully, folded it back up, and after having thought it over for a while, she sighed and said, "Well, at least we had a good time."

It was almost dark and there was no one else in the park. It must have been dinner time. Then suddenly, we saw Miss Morty coming toward us, looking stranger than ever.

"He told me I'd find you here," she said.

"Who told you?" I asked.

"Your ancestor the pirate. I'd just sat down at the table with a nice bowl of soup when I heard his voice. He asked me to come here and bring you a message from him. If another ghost had asked me I would've told him to wait until after dinner, but he's such a nice guy that I decided to do as he asked."

"Let's hear this message," I said without excessive enthusiasm.

"Aren't you happy to receive an urgent communiqué from the great beyond?"

"I don't share your sympathies for my progenitor."

"In any case, the message is really cute because it's all in rhyme. Was your ancestor a poet as well?"

"He was involved in the arts all right - the art of the swindle. If he'd been a painter he would have specialized in *trompe l'oeil*."

"Oh, well, at any rate, this here's the message: 'The last of the lines and none but these, to the treasure you want these are the keys.' And now if you'll excuse me I'll get back to my dinner. I wouldn't want my soup to get too cold."

That said, she executed a perfect turn and walked away in her usual serpentine manner.

Once we were alone again, Lorelai asked, "Which last lines? The ones in the message?"

Seeing as it was still in my hand, I unfolded it and read the final part of it again out loud: "When in your home once again you will be, if in the evening your sleep's slow in coming, look for the blackcap and hear what he's saying."

After having mulled it over for a bit, she said, "Who knows what it means."

"It means absolutely nothing," I cut short. "I'm certainly not about to start listening to every stupid little bird that passes by just to give that old scoundrel a few laughs."

"I'm sorry, my angry little sweetie pie, but I don't agree! First of all, those little birds you talk about aren't stupid at all and listening to them, especially the blackcaps, is always delightful; and what's more, it may be that there's a secret hidden in these words."

"Listen, if we simply refuse to find fault with One-Eyed Buck, I can only suppose that he had a split personality - one side pirate and the other a sort of poet-philosopher - who came to the conclusion that listening to birds sing is the only real treasure this life has to offer us. But now let's put it out of our minds. We'd best be getting home - there's a full moon and I wouldn't want to run into Robert, the werewolf."

I always tried to avoid clashing with Robert because we were friends. The fact that I was his friend, didn't spare me from his attacks, however, for when he was transformed he made no distinctions and jumped on anyone who came within range. Everyone was afraid of him, though my fear in this case was that I might hurt him, since as the monster Grunz I was much stronger than he was.

We were happy to return home at last and get back to the old routine, because while the trip had certainly been great fun, it had also been a bit intense. There were many habits Lorelai and I shared, and one of these was to never to leave things unfinished. So as soon we

got inside, we immediately set about conclu-
ding our Nau-Nau ritual that had been interrupted so suddenly on that lovely Hawaiian
beach. Then, following a light dinner and a few
games of table tennis, we went up to the tower
to admire the moon until our need for sleep
convinced us to turn in.

Although it was wonderful to be back in my
own bed, I had trouble falling asleep. Not Lorelai, however, who'd fallen into the arms of Mor-
pheus as soon as her head hit the pillow.

As I usually did in such cases, I gazed up at
the gorgeous fresco on the ceiling of our room,
which depicted an idyllic rural landscape popu-
lated by strapping young farmers and delightful
peasant girls in celebration, surrounded by an
infinite variety of animals. I could do so because when we were at home, we never went to
sleep in total darkness. We preferred to leave a
couple of lit candles which would extinguish
themselves during the night. The flickering
candlelight seemed to bring the figures in the
fresco to life, creating a truly unique effect.

And that's when I saw it, high up on the left.
Undoubtedly it had always been there, but I'd
never noticed it. On the other hand, why
should I ever have noticed a little blackcap poi-
sed on a tree branch in a landscape so crowded with men, women and animals? I looked
more carefully and I realized that from its
beak, open as if in song, there emerged a sort
of gilded ribbon on which some words were

written, as if the painter had wished to make it speak. I jumped down from the bed and ran to turn the light on despite Lorelai's protests. When I told her what I'd discovered, she too snapped wide awake. I took a stepladder and climbed up to go see what the little blackcap had to tell us. The ceiling was more than five meters above the ground and thus not easy to reach, I was nevertheless able to get close enough to read what interested me.

And this is what that dark-feathered little bird had been chirping up there for around four-hundred years: "Even if about me you've had more than a doubt / that for which you've searched shall now be found out / No more complaints, let no more tears swell / rather run now you must, and look down the well."

Now there was no really use in One-Eyed Buck getting bent out of shape just because I'd doubted him!

Well, yes, I had thought it was all a trick, but he and his mysterious messages had to accept their share of the blame. And anyway, I'd never really complained all that much. Or maybe I had, but I'd certainly never reached the point of tears. I wondered how he'd managed to predict my loss of faith in him. It almost seemed that he'd deliberately provoked it in order to play the victim afterwards.

While I was mulling these things over, Lorelai asked me from down below, "So, my tongue-tied little sweetie pie, what's written up there?"

I came down and shared with her the black-cap's message. Our thoughts immediately raced to the old stone well down in the house's inner courtyard, dry for centuries and sealed for just as long by a heavy iron cover.
Still in our pajamas, we raced down the wide staircase, reached the courtyard, and unsealed the well - though not without some difficulty. It was full halfway to the top with gold coins. Predictably, Lorelai began to dance around laughing. Then she embraced me, kissing me with lips smothered not in the usual lipstick, but this time in chapstick.

www.ingramcontent.com/pod-product-compliance
Lightning Source LLC
Chambersburg PA
CBHW020624130626
46552CB00003B/1088

* 9 7 8 8 8 9 4 0 3 0 4 2 6 *